Shopping

I Love Shopping

By Lauren Cook

Nightboat Books
New York

ISBN: 978-1-64362-286-6

I Love Shopping was first published by
glo worm press in 2019.

Design and typesetting by Lauren Cook
and Rissa Hochberger
Typeset in Times New Roman

Cataloging-in-publication data is available
from the Library of Congress

Nightboat Books
New York
www.nightboat.org

I love God and I love things
I love shopping
But right now
I'm mad at the mall

It is so dark here at night. When it is dark like this, it is also very light. When there are no street lights and a big open sky you can really see how much light that big open sky makes. The tree line is dark and ragged and even when I take off my glasses and can't see much at all through my bedroom window, the stars still can reach me. They take the form of blurred circles. When I wake up in the morning, I wake up early. I feed the chickens and I check on the plants and harvest them before the afternoon sun takes all their oils out with the heat. At dusk, I water them and let the chickens back in for the night.

I got the lead role in the school play. I have always wanted to be an actor. I'm very good at lying. I'm very good at pretending. Maybe children make such good actors sometimes because there is more of a blur between what is real and what isn't. Adult actors I think always know that they are pretending and that everyone is laughing at them and their desperate choices. That feeling isn't specific to actors though. I'm not trying to say everyone always thinks everyone is laughing at them, but I do think everyone is always making desperate choices towards a promise of more. There are many things you are not told as a child. Maybe those things you don't know really help you to live in a space between the two worlds. You know enough to know that you are saying what you are told to say, that the words are not your own, but maybe you don't know enough that it just feels like your life. Like, if you pick up an animal and put it down somewhere else it will just keep living its life in that new spot.

My mommy told me that chickens have collective souls. She thinks all chickens feel individually and experience different lives, and that is an inescapable truth, but that in general all chickens are one massive soul that inhabits different bodies. She doesn't mean to diminish their existences. She means it to make their existences more potent, more powerful. After a long time, I sort of agree. Although I think it is the type of logic that could be dangerous if it fell into the wrong hands. We are very married to the idea that souls are what give life value. I feel like I was told that each thing having an individual soul is the reason this life is so beautiful and special to so many people. What my mom is trying to say is that the collective soul is what makes their lives so beautiful and special. That's what she sees when she looks at a group of chickens and sees them as one. They are one. They got here all together. We have many ways to describe and name the things we do not understand. Sometimes just listening to what someone told you is enough of a religion for me.

the moon was big last night and the owls were
screaming and the coyotes were screaming and

I have thought the reason thereof to be this, that
they wrote surely in strawberry time.

Accessories are the candy of clothes

Soothing effect on emotions, particularly jealousy,
grief, and resentment. Useful for all skin types.
Especially mature, dry, hard, or sensitive skin.

Venus's looking glass
Hairy honeysuckle
The sexiest girl I know
Quietly snores

Starting fires from beyond the grave
Only trusting when they say something ominous
Broad leaved spring beauty
An egg with two yolks
Racing a pack of migrating birds
I am no good at sitting on something...

Think about all the animals that love sugar like we
do

When you pick seafoam up it turns into water
I miss the spider living in the port-a-potty

Honey brim Rd
Ox cart Rd
I live in the muddle of nowhere

The cookie crumbles, but it also rebuilds

All along the gates to the back entrance there are presumably planted *Rosa rugosa* bushes. I don't think they're sprayed because they appear to not be taken care of in that way. They are not trimmed, and are growing up instead of out, which indicates they are not thought of often (pruned.) Only the grass around them is mowed. These bushes produce the largest rosehips I've ever seen. Probably about an inch and a half in width. They look like big cherry tomatoes.

I almost hit a bear that crossed the street while I was driving on the backroads around there.

We saw a baby porcupine in a tree.

On the drive home we saw a skunk, a fox, and an orange cat.

I respect the way they let you park anywhere up and down that river, through those mountains, so you can get in that river and swim. They know how hot it is.

Can't wait to eat bread by the river. I will jump in the river.

I am the dog of a beautiful person. I am a small dog, with a robust body. When you tap on the side of me I make a good noise. I have a cute and sweet face. My breath smells bad, but I have a very endearing personality. The beautiful person loves me. I love them too. I love everyone I meet. I am a dog and I get what I need from the people around me so, I am ok. I feel full of love all the time. I try to spread that love as often as I can.

I do not know how long I have been alive. I don't really remember what has happened to me before this moment except in feeling. I know the range of emotions I can feel. I can remember the pain of the bad time. But I cannot remember faces. It is like when you can only remember the feeling of a dream, how it made you feel. Everything is simultaneously old and new with me. I respond to what is in front of me. My first response and reaction is love. I love to eat and sleep and to be close to my friends.

Here is my kinky roleplay:

I am an honest person. I am not ashamed of myself, the things I do, the things I create. This makes my life very easy to live. I do not have to lie or withhold truth from the people I love and who love me. I just get up and live my truth. I am a nice person who does decent things. I mind my business. I find happiness in small things. It is very easy for me. I love my morning coffee. I love the sunrise and the sunset. I love to go on weekend vacations with my friends. These things make me happy. When the sun sets at night, a deep feeling of anxiety does not wash over me. I am very lucky and happy. When people say nice things about me, I hear them and they soak into me. I have everything I need in this life.

reanimating after being out in the cold

I'm such a spoiled brat
I live like 50 feet from an apple tree that got
struck by lightning and split in two and I never
think about that much. I'm so ungrateful

I am the part of the ground that does not get
touched by dew

Every year at least one person drowns in The
Neversink River
You can read about it in the local paper

Goodnight dry quarry
I can climb on your rocks No More

sucking on a piece of ancient amber
like candy

Did you know sometimes earthworms can eat TOO much soil?

I'm just thinking about all the flowers on curved back roads with low, deep shoulders and no place to pull over so you can't even pull over to see them.

Trees can make me feel psychotic because I'm trained to think I am never alone except when I'm with the trees. You're not really alone when it is just you and the trees, but everyone tells me that's what being alone is. Everyone is like, being alone is with like, trees. Out there. Separate from us.

When the ticks wake up and crawl out of the darkest, blackest soil I have ever seen. Bobbi said ticks don't die in the winter, they just live under the snow.

honestly I'm in the mood to chop some wood,
but there's no wood to chop

I wake up in the middle of the night to write
down "tamed grass"

My Own Privates
and for that I'm sorry
I have a barbed tongue
and I haven't been here since I was robbed many
years ago
you weren't there, but I think I vaguely told you
and you were empathetic
but there's only so much

Trans masc names:
Spud
Pepper
Soup
Swatch
Mirror
Bats

My crazy idea is that evolutionarily there is some benefit to being materialistic because something developed in our brains to make us enjoy acquiring objects because of hunting and gathering...like it would be an evolutionary benefit to enjoy collecting objects because we have to collect food and feel attracted to food in the same way animals are....so we like shopping because shopping replaced foraging...just a theory though.

Betrayal mix

I'm having fun eating saltines

On New Years Eve of 2014-2015 I saw Lindsay Lohan in Chinatown. It was a good year. She was in a black SUV and I was on the sidewalk and she had her window rolled down.

On New Year's Eve of 2016-2017 I saw a raccoon eating persimmons out of a tree in someone's backyard. Both of these things feel the same to me and mean the same thing.

Doing things jokingly is a gateway drug to doing thing sincerely

A competition to see who can find beauty in the most obscure thing

Most people decide that new pain is the solution to keeping them from thinking about old pain

I think it would be really cool to use a ceramic teapot as a purse

I've always wanted to name a dog "onion." You could call her sweet onion.

The only time I can pace myself is when I pretend it's a character I'm playing

The Pink Lady Slipper Orchid

Introduction

Lady Slipper orchids, of the genus *Cypripedium*, are the subject of much fascination. Their comparative availability as a wild orchid in America makes them widely known. Lady slippers are the state flower of Minnesota and the Provincial flower of Prince Edward Island, Canada. Lady slippers can be a common orchid with sometimes great local abundance that grows over the span of a larger geographical area, but they are still generally at risk and rare. Their choice of habitat is most of Eastern North America. Because of their specificity as a species their dispersal potential is limited. Their seeds are difficult to germinate.They take a very long time to flower, they require very specific mycorrhizal fungi to grow, and very specific pollinators to pollinate them. They are particularly vulnerable to sporadic or cyclical ecological events. What does the lady slipper orchid need? How can we give them what they need in order to ensure future generations get to meet them too?

History & Conservation Attempts

The genus *Cypripedium* comes from the Greek word "Kypris," which is a name for Venus/Aphrodite. The suffix comes from "pedion," which is Greek in reference to feet. This name translates roughly to Venus' shoe. The plant family Orchidaceae has the highest proportion of threatened genera, containing many threatened species (Swarts et al., 2009). Orchids are either epiphytes, lithophytes, or terrestrial. Lady slippers are terrestrial orchids, meaning they grow from the ground. Half of the extinct plant species are terrestrial her-baceous perennials (The World Conservation Union,1999). Terrestrial orchids are at a greater extinction risk. In general the highly specialized evolution of orchids has made them interesting and increasingly diverse, but this also puts them at high risk because they depend on many synchronized factors for their success. The proof of their elusive-ness is shown in the amount of time and effort people put into either conserving or collect-ing orchids. In Rhode Island, the last known orchid plant of *Orchis spectabilis* was eaten by a skunk during the night (Stuckey et al., 1967). The fate of many orchids relies on simply

hoping that random ecological events, including human interference and development, do
not destroy populations. Orchids are also a
highly fetishized plant with high commodity
market value. They are often collected for
profit. According to Swarts and Dixon in their
2009 paper *Terrestrial orchid conservation in
the age of extinction*, "The nature of threaten-
ing processes to orchids in almost all cases can
be traced to human activities, including land
clearing for agriculture, mining, urban development, weed invasion, grazing, altered environmental conditions and collection of plants
for horticulture and ethnobotanical purpose."
During the mid-1800s until the first World War
there was a "golden age" of plant collecting,
where the jungles of Brazil, Colombia, Burma,
Borneo, and New Guinea were ravaged for
various orchid species (Swarts et al 2009).
Although orchids have more protection than
ever, illegal collection still occurs.

In Britain, *Cypripedium calceolus* was
a rare orchid. By 1917, it was thought to
be extinct from overcollection by botanists
and gardeners, until one plant was rediscov-
ered in the 1930s. By 1950, there was only
one natural site of lady slipper orchids left
(Ramsay et al., 1998). This site has remained

intact and began being consciously protected in the 1970s. Because the lady slipper was being removed, and not dying off from changes in their habitats, there have been many success-ful conservation attempts to reintroduce them into the wild. Scientists from the Sainsbury Orchid Conservation Project, the Royal Botanic Gardens, and English Nature have transplanted flowers back into the wild and hand pollinated them for years. Successful re-establishment is defined as the population being able to sustain itself, but for now the lady slippers in Britain still require human help. The goal is to eventu-ally have the lady slipper return in abundance.

Mycorrhizal fungi

Lady Slipper orchids are often found grow-ing with pine trees but can also be found in mixed-hardwood coniferous forests. They are often associated with acidic, calcium rich soil. Local folklore and colloquial knowledge also says that lady slippers come up after brush fires. Peak lady slipper orchid bloom is usually thought to be 10-15 years after a fire (Stuckey et al., 1967). Lady slipper orchid seeds are specks of dust. The fungus finds its way into the embryo of the seed and grows into its cells, forming pelotons (Ramsay et al., 1998). The seed then develops into a protocorm underground, which is a tuberous collection of cells common in various young orchids. After one to many years, the lady slipper orchid lengthens its rhizome and sprouts as a seedling. The plant is able to flower usually three years after it germinates. Lady slipper orchids are known for their tendency to undergo adult whole-plant dormancy (Shefferson et al., 2007). This is a condition in which the plant does not sprout for a year or more at a time, leading many to believe that during this time the lady slipper orchid depends heavily on its mycorrhizal relationships to carry it through. Overall though, mature lady slipper orchids are understood to rely less on their fungal partners compared to the importance of the fungal presence in germination and early life.

In the wild, mycorrhizal fungi are necessary for the germination and growth of orchid seeds. This mycorrhizal relationship involves the transference of carbon and other nutrients between plant and fungal partner (Bunch et al., 2013). Orchid seeds require carbon, nitrogen, and other nutrition from fungus. Even after the plant germinates and begins to photosynthesize, the orchid still remains reliant on the fungus. Most types of mycorrhizal relationships are mutualistic, meaning the plant and the fungus exchange nutrients. Orchids often are parasitic, taking nutrition and offering the fungus nothing in return.

A study conducted focusing on the pink lady slipper orchid, *Cypripedium acaule*, published in the journal *Botany* in 2013 sampled root and soils from 70 plants across 16 populations in the state of Georgia. Soil was extracted around each plant by using 3 centimeter diameter soil probes. Six probes took samples at approximately 10 cm deep and about 12 cm from the base of each plant. Four roots were removed from each plant and put on ice. Roots were surface sterilized in the lab and each root was cut in 3 centimeter sections. The sections were viewed under a microscope for the presence of pelotons, which are "hyphal coils within the cells of the plant root cortex that are the key evidence of orchid mycorrhizal colonization."

Soil content was variable, with the only consistent thing being the presence of carbon. Soil pH was also consistently low and acidic at all sites, varying from 4.18 +/- 0.05. According to this study, calcium was interestingly the least consistent environmental factor.

Information on the fungus was extracted through PCR amplification. 61 out of the 70 plants sampled were viable and 133 of the 250 roots were viable. Out of 133 root samples, 74 were repeats or a fungus that only occurred once. This study found 53 different fungal taxa on the roots of pink lady slipper orchids. Only 15 of these species occurred in more than one plant. *Tulasnella* and *Russula* fungi were the most commonly found, specifically *Tulasnella tomaculum* and *Russula laccata*. The fungi found more than once includes *Cadophora finlandica, Cistella spiciola, Cladopgialophoa chaetospira, Diaporthe phaseolorum, Lactarius imperceptus, Meliniomyces variabilis, Oidiodendron maius, Phialea strobilina, Phialocephala fortinii, R. laccata, R. virescens, Sorocybe resinae, Tulasnella asymmetric, T. pruinosa,* and *T. tomaculum. Tulasnella asymmetric, T. tomaculum,* and *T. pruinosa* had all previously been documented and established as fungi that have mycorrhizal relationships with orchids. *Russula* have also been linked to orchids, along with *Phialocephala* and *Cadophora.*

Although many have been able to name fungi that have relationships with lady slippers, we still don't necessarily know why the orchids choose the fungus they do. Maybe the fungus chooses the orchid. Some studies believe lady slipper orchids decide with which mycorrhizal fungi to form relationships. Orchid protocorms have been seen directly manipulating their host fungi once their original contact is initiated (Shefferson et al., 2007). Many believe this manipulation implies that there is an adaptive advantage to the orchid making a choice. Many believe that more information is needed on the fungi that the lady slipper is often associated with, specifically *Russula* and *Tulasnella.* Most scientists believed that *Tulasnella* was only a saprotrophic mushroom until the publishing of multiple studies in 2003 that disprove this, but its relationship with the lady slipper is mycorrhizal. Mycorrhizal relationships are thought to vary widely over large geographic spans and similar studies should be conducted in various locations with various populations. The 2013 study from *Botany* concludes, "Though there is clearly a relationship between the soil environment and fungal associate identity, it is unclear whether this relationship is determined by fungal distribution, selection by the orchid, or both. It is hard for scientists to be able to really prove the lady slipper makes distinct fungal partner choices, although this theory is quite harmonious and pleasing.

Pollination

The pink lady slipper is mostly pollinated by queen bumblebees (O'Connell et al., 1998). Insects enter through the fissure on the front lip and leave through the base of the lip. The insect can not exit through the hole it entered. This makes the insect pass by the stigma and brush past the anthers. Although pink lady slippers are bright and sweet smelling, they produce no nectar. Lady slipper orchids are deceptive orchids. This means that they produce no reward for pollinators. It is estimated that out of the 180,000-300,000 species of orchids on Earth, about one third of them produce no rewards (O'Connell et al., 1998). Species number and diversity in flower structure in orchids is often attributed to them having a very specific pollinator and many orchids have very specific pollinators. The lady slipper is less reliant on one specific pollinator. Non-rewarding species of orchids are thought to be mostly trafficked by "inexperienced pollinators." This means that the pollinator would go to the lady slipper less over time as

28

it learns that there is no nectar being supplied in exchange. This sort of means that the lady slipper is accidentally, or non-intentionally pollinated. It is performed by whoever happens to be there and willing to try.

Non-rewarding orchids are known infamously for their low pollination success in the wild. Although lady slippers show success through hand pollination, natural circumstantial pollination shows alarmingly low fruit rates. In a 1998 study published by O'Connell and Johnston called *Male and female pollination success in a deceptive orchid, a selection study*, 100% of their hand-pollinated *Cypripedium acaule* produced fruit, but only 5% and 13% of the non-hand-pollinated orchids produced fruit. It is important to keep in mind though that because orchids are perennials that live for long periods of time, the pollinator selection of one year cannot represent the pollinator activity of other years. There are other factors that contribute to the success of the insect population, like water, temperature, etc. Lady slipper orchids grow in woodlands where pollinators have a harder time accessing them.

Non-rewarding orchids have a much higher chance of being pollinated in nature if they are surrounded by plants that do reward pollinators. In O'Connell and Johnston's study, lady slipper orchids had the highest success when surrounded by ericaceous shrubs, particularly blueberry and huckleberry, with an open tree canopy. Ericaceous shrubs enjoy the same type of conditions as lady slippers. The bumblebees that pollinate the lady slippers come to heir microhabitat for the blueberry flowers, and casually find themselves in the lady slipper orchids. A study of *Cypripedium* that took place on Oland in Sweden revealed that weather conditions and the presence of rewarding flowers nearby affect the outcome of lady slipper pollination the most (Ramsay et al., 1998).

Conclusion

After a history of overcollection, hopefully heightened awareness and increasing shifts in public interest towards preserving biodiversity can help create conditions for a future where the lady slipper orchid is still present. Conservation of forests and protection of lady slipper habitats will be imperative moving forward, both specifically for the lady slipper but also for the general health of our ecosystems.

Systems of reintroduction have proven to be successful, but taking steps now to protect known sites is important. Lady slippers seemingly appear to need a lot—a series of random, off-chance, coincidental conditions must all line up for the lady slipper to naturally germinate, flower, and fruit. This terrestrial orchid is difficult, but that's exactly what makes it so special to see them growing in the woods all on their own, to stumble upon a site.

Works Cited

Nies, A. (2013). Nutrient availability of white lady's slipper orchids (Cypripedium candidum) affects presence of mycorrhizal partners Geralle Powell, Wellesley College.

Shefferson, R. P., WEIß, M. I. C. H. A. E. L., Kull, T. I. I. U., & Taylor, D. (2005). High specificity generally characterizes mycorrhizal association in rare lady's slipper orchids, genus Cypripedium. *Molecular Ecology*, 14(2), 613-626.

RAMSAY, M. M., & Stewart, J. (1998). Re-establishment of the lady's slipper orchid (Cypripedium calceolus L.) in Britain. *Botanical Journal of the Linnean Society, 126*(1-2), 173-181.

What are Pollinators? (n.d.). Retrieved from http://www.pollinator.org/pollination

O'Connell, L. M., & Johnston, M. O. (1998). Male and female pollination success in a deceptive orchid, a selection study. *Ecology*, 79(4), 1246-1260.

Shefferson, R. P., Taylor, D. L., Weiß, M., Garnica, S., McCormick, M. K., Adams, S., ... & Yukawa, T. (2007). The evolutionary history of mycorrhizal specificity among lady's slipper orchids. *Evolution*, 61(6), 1380-1390.

Stuckey, I. H. (1967). Environmental factors and the growth of native orchids. *American Journal of Botany*, 232-241.

Swarts, N. D., & Dixon, K. W. (2009). Terrestrial orchid conservation in the age of extinction. *Annals of Botany*, 104(3), 543-556.

Caryopsis, J. (n.d.). Pink Lady's Slipper (Cypripedium acaule). Retrieved from http://www.naturenorth.com/spring/flora/pladysl/Fplady2.html

Bunch, W. D., Cowden, C. C., Wurzburger, N., & Shefferson, R. P. (2013). Geography and soil chemistry drive the distribution of fungal associations in lady's slipper orchid, Cypripedium acaule. *Botany*, 91(12), 850-856.

Nature Posts. (n.d.). Retrieved November 29, 2017, from http://www.abundantnature.com/2011/05/pink-ladys-slipper-dupes-bees.html

I do not know of a single hell that is not personal.

Someone sitting and smiling to themselves and someone walks by and smiles back and the person sitting says, "Oh no I was just trying to check and see if I was having a stroke."

I am the world's best ballerina. I have been working at this my whole life. I am 16 years old and dance is my life. I went to dance camp. All my friends are dancers. We smoke cigarettes. Oftentimes, I don't feel alive. The sick and dedicated, among others I can not think of off the top of my head, talk to god all the time...asking god to deliver gifts. Progress CAN be pain but that doesn't mean progress IS pain. When I talk to God I ask them to make me the best dancer that will ever exist. the best dancer that this world has EVER known.

I am a writer and just now I think I realized for the first time, if you write about your fantasies it is like they happened to you and you can move on. It takes me a really long time to realize important stuff that is imperative to my happiness but no time at all to remember things that don't matter. I know exactly where you left your keys. They are on the floor under the right, front leg of your desk. You put them on the desk when you came in, but they fell off onto the floor

I'm the best scientist in the world. I'm 43 years old. I got them to ban plastic everywhere. I wear a big lab coat everyday and safety goggles and gloves. I'm really smart. I went to college for like, 10 years. Right now, I am working on a new way to end all suffering. I will keep you updated.

I have worn
your suede Miu Miu loafers in the chicken coop
that were in
the bedroom

and which
you were probably
saving
for casual daytime looks

Forgive me
they got chicken shit all over the bottom
so rude of me
and so stinky

I think the best thing I am good at is having thoughts. I'm really good at thinking of stuff. It isn't necessarily smart stuff, I'm not saying that. I just mean thinking is a big hobby of mine. It takes up a lot of my time whether I like it or not. I'm actually not that good at having thoughts. My thoughts can be really bad a lot of the time. I don't like my thoughts, but I have many, many thoughts. And that makes me good at it, because I have them and I'm constantly working at it.

Lies are incredible at bringing people together
but so is truth

I listen to my friends talk about their feelings
I feel like I don't have any feelings when I listen
to other people talk about their feelings.

When people are talking to me, I'm like, I wish
I was writing and when I'm writing, I'm like, oh
God, I wish people were talking to me. In my
world, writing is a synonym for anything I am
doing. When I do anything, I am writing because
I believe that even just having thoughts that are
sentences is writing.

I wonder if heaven will have the skateboarders I
kissed in middle school

Jennifer on *Top Chef* said that whoever thought
a snail looked good to eat must have been really
fucking hungry

I check Instagram stories and I see that the same
storm over me is the same storm over you

I think it is kinda cool that humans can't really
predict the weather that good. The weather is the
top and we are the bottom

I am attracted to the air. I am an airsexual. When the wind blows on me hard, I cum. It feels so good. That is why I am so horny all the time. I don't need a job because I am so happy. I have a house with a backyard and there's a big hill and I sit on a folding chair on top of the hill where the wind blows all day and I cum over and over again and that is my purpose.

I said my toe hurt because my toenail fell off and you said just focus on another part of your body, put your attention somewhere else, so I focused on my other foot and my toe hurt less. I said, how could you keep that secret from me? How could you have never told me that trick? You have so many secrets and you said, what? I don't have secrets and I said, no! Secrets are anything you haven't told me yet, not just like, I kissed the butler, but like, the other day I dipped a pickle in mayonnaise and ate it, or that you can use an alligator hair clip as a chip clip. A secret is anything you haven't told me.

A "honey hole" is a term that refers to a location that will provide a commodity or resource. "I found a honey hole" / "I found a honey hole of _____" means to have found a surplus of goods. This term can refer to foraging, hunting, fishing, antiquing.

If I'm high as shit and I see the moon, like, for the first time in the night especially if she looks really good I'm gonna wave and say, "Hi" like, sorry, I can't help it.

I am 32 years old. I went to school for engi-
neering. My dad bought me a Mustang when
I was 16. I wear gingham print shirts from
Brooks Brothers tucked into chinos with boat
shoes. I get my haircut every week from the
same guy, every week for 6 years. I used to
live in the city, but I saved up and bought a
house Upstate. I saved up a lot of money engi-
neering for so many years. Now I have a truck.
There are a lot of strip malls but also open
fields. I still commute to the city for work, but
me and my wife enjoy the country life. I take
pictures of her for her Instagram. She loves to
wear wide brim hats, with long flowing dresses
while standing in fields of flowers. She has 50k
followers. I love to drive my truck around. I'm
not gay, but I like to get my dick sucked by
men. I don't know why and I don't think about
it or care to think about it. It just is what it is.
I have Grindr and my profile is blank and the
text just says "looking to get my dick sucked"
and I just message everyone I like until I find
someone to suck my dick. I send pictures when
people ask. I love getting my dick sucked in
my truck. I love the way the windows fog
up. The best part is finding a place to park. I
always position the car so the windshield has
a view of something. It can't always happen

perfectly, because oftentimes, I have to drive around to different places to pick up the men, but my favorite spot is this one that overlooks the entire city. At night it is so beautiful.

In the locker room everyone is so fucking scared of being gay. I am 12 years old. I am in 6th grade. I'm not even gay, but I'm so sick and tired of everyone being scared of being gay. I had to learn this way to change clothes that makes it so you don't expose yourself at all to anyone. You put your shorts over your pants and you take your pants off under the shorts. You put your tank top over your shirt and you take the shirt off under the tank top. You can't look at anyone's body. I don't think there is anything wrong with looking at each other's bodies. I don't want to look unnecessarily, but I want to be able to move my eyes freely around the room without being scared of accidentally looking at someone's body. When I was 10 and I was in camp we would strip naked before we went swimming in the bunk and dance with each other. I watched this girl make-out with a poster we had of Usher while we all cheered her on. Now I'm here in 6th grade and it seems like a major regression.

I have been eating candy for as long as I can remember. I love gummies first, then chocolate, then all the other candies. I love ice cream and cakes and donuts. I eat sweets all day everyday. I don't brush my teeth either. I don't believe in brushing my teeth. I have never even seen dental floss before. I went to the dentist because I was scared my teeth were going to fall out. I was scared I was making a huge mistake. He told me I had the best teeth he has ever seen in his life. He called everyone else working into the exam room to look at my teeth, to see how beautiful they were. It was the most special I ever felt in my life. On the drive home, after getting my perfect teeth cleaned and congratulated, I thought to myself that this must be what it feels like to win the lottery.

I have the best boyfriend in the world. He is 6'2".
In the summer, he wears a white tank top with
jeans and white sneakers. In the winter, he wears
a long sleeve white thermal waffle shirt and
jeans with black boots. His winter coat is black
and down. He smells like onions. He has big
knuckles. He has big feet. His fingers look like
sausages kind of. He only eats beans from a can
and drinks Dr. Pepper. I don't try to get him to
eat anything else. I don't care if he eats healthy.
We go to the bar sometimes. We sit at the bar and
he orders my drink for me and we drink together
until we are both sort of drunk. He pays attention
to me but also isn't obsessed with me, which is
a nice balance I think. I try to convince him to
dance, but he won't do it. I think it is stupid that
he doesn't dance.

If you are nice, you can just say to yourself over and over again, I am worthy of love because I am nice and nice people are the best

hey guys! i'm currently trying to invent something! send me any ideas if you have any!

I am in love with a girl who sneezes all the time.
We fell in love because she went to sneeze and
I put my finger under her nose. Everytime she is
about to sneeze, I put my finger under her nose
to catch it. She sneezes like, once every minute.
It makes her happy to have someone anticipating
her needs like that. I love to tend to her and make
her happy. I love her sneezing on my finger. Even
when she sleeps she sneezes. When people stare
at us in public, I make faces at them. Stop staring
at me and my beautiful girlfriend who sneezes all
the time.

I KNOW THAT I WILL ONLY CHANGE
THROUGH THE PASSAGE OF TIME AND
THE LEARNING OF LESSONS.
AND THAT ALL THE PARTS OF ME
I CHOOSE TO FIXATE ON ARE JUST
DISTRACTIONS TO KEEP ME FROM
DOING THE SOUL CRUSHING WORK OF
_____. WHATEVER. ANYTHING. THE SOUL
CRUSHING WORK OF ANYTHING. ALL
WORK IS SOUL CRUSHING.

Here is an impression of someone in denial:
I am not in denial

> Hey
>> What's Up?
> Not much
>> You haven't signed on in awhile...I thought you were mad at me
> No, I just have been busy
>> Too busy for me?
> I'm sorry. I think about you all the time
>> I think about you all the time. You're all I think about.
>> Why don't you call? You have my number. I try calling you
> I've just been busy. I go to school and I go to work. I barely have time for myself.
>> I know...but I'm always here
> I know
>> Do you know what I think about?
> What?
>> Your voice. I think about your voice on the phone when I touch myself
> Really?
>> Yes...I think about your late night whisper voice
> That's so hot
>> Yeah?
> Yea...that makes me hard just thinking about it.
>> I think about what it would be like if we met one day...all the things I would do to you

> Yea?

>> Yea...and I think about all the things you're doing in the world when you're not talking to me. I like to imagine you at school or work or out being a slut and it makes me feel so hot.

> Yea?

>> Yeah...and I like to think about showing up one day outside where you work and surprising you and taking you right there.

> Fuck...that's so hot

>> Send me a picture of yourself

> Ok

> IMG_422.JPG

>> Fuck...you look so hot.

I am 10 years old. I live on an old farm on a county road. My school is 45 minutes from where I live. There are 15 kids in my class. I have two friends. My friends all live far away and my mom won't drive me anywhere. My brothers are older than me so they aren't fun. They just yell at me. My mom is working. That is why she can't drive me. I sit on the computer and talk to kids around the world all day. When I am not on the computer, I am watching TV or I go sit outside and pretend I am in a music video. I put my headphones in and walk around the field and make faces at the pretend cameras. Sometimes I read books. In my head I make up people to write letters to and I write letters and stick them in the holes of trees. I got this idea because I read a book about a girl who writes letters to her grandma and leaves them in the hole of a tree and her grandma writes back. She and her grandma live in a big pink house in a town where people live next to each other. I think about how much better I would be if I lived near people. I don't like riding my bike on the county road so I ride my bike up and down the driveway and pretend different spots on my driveway are different stores and people's houses. Under each tree is different. The barn is my house. I climb on the hay bales and pretend it is my bed.

I am just 10 years old so I'm trying not to pre-emptively start a mythology about myself, but I am magic. I know all the words to my favorite songs and I want to sing in front of arenas of people one day. I want a fashion line and I want to help save the elephants.

In my dream last night, there was honeysuckle.
I was trying to hide two dead bodies. I found the
two dead bodies and for some reason felt like it
was my responsibility to hide them. I felt like I
couldn't tell anyone about them because I was
scared I would ruin my life. When I was pan-
icking, out of my peripheral vision I saw honeysuckle. In my dream, I thought to myself, wow,
that's so special. Today while I was walking the
rich people's dog for money, I walked down an
alley I don't usually walk down and saw honeysuckle growing over a fence. It is late October.
Honeysuckle usually blooms in the spring. It
must be flowering this late because it was cut
back before it got to go to seed. Now I'm like,
maybe there is always honeysuckle in the periph-
ery. I watch a white moth fly side by side, in a
zigzag motion, over the head of the rich person's
dog like a hawk flying over a car. I'm in love
with the dog, but he belongs to rich people. He is
the best dog I have ever met.

I'm really obsessed with the things I don't know lately or can't see. Like when we all say, good-night, we all go sit in separate rooms until when-ever we see each other again. I like to imagine people I know waking up and washing their faces and drinking their coffee. Like who are you before we are meeting up to talk? What is your morning piss like?

It is so crazy that scientists want to try to find ways to live forever when nobody is even going to want to do that anyway because being alive runs parallel to suffering with no alley in between.

I will focus on what I like and not what I don't like

I will not sleep all day

I will say yes more

Hi readers! Welcome back to my blog. I just want to thank everyone who is still reading despite the long hiatus I took this year. I just felt like I couldn't blog anymore. I felt like I couldn't think of any new ideas. I felt like I wanted to go back to living my days for me, not for the internet. I spent a lot of time alone, just soul searching. But now, I'm back. And I want to share with you my new knitting patterns and pictures of my dog's birthday party. It wasn't a big party, really, just a few of us, but we got her a dog cake and watched a dog movie. I also dyed my hair during the hiatus. I bleached it and got purple tips. I really feel like a new person. Thank you for supporting me.

My step-dad yells at me for denting my car and
calls me irresponsible

I say, hey man, the difference between me and you
is I can love something even though it is ugly

I said I love you baby fairy and you said awww
wow yes I am a fairy wow aww yea

and you looked at me and said you're my bed of
moss!

I said yea thats where we are on a bed of moss she
said

No! You're the bed of moss I said ohhh...I couldn't
hear you....

you said I sleep on you I snuggle up on you

I said I can't believe in your fantasy I am your bed

Pulverized sidewalk asphalt fated fallen fruit
is not that different than its brother, the com-
postable material that sits in landfills and doesn't
rot, crying methane forever

For some reason when I decide something is
right or wrong, even if it happened long ago,
maybe someone told me as a child, it is hard
to change my mind. I get so caught up in these
ideas of what is right or wrong in a way that
hinders my success. I know the truth. I know that
everything is nuanced so there isn't really a right
or wrong in interpersonal matters. I know what
the correct answer is. I know that progress and
occurrences are not linear but meshes and webs
and all that theory stuff. But I can only think
about things like, oh this is tarnished forever
after one thing goes wrong. Or like, *oh we aren't
supposed to do that.*

Another problem I have is that I think all my
problems are my problems and that there isn't
a single person in the world who has to know
what I'm going through because it is unfair to
expect people to help you when everyone has
their own problems. I know this is also not true.
I get very stressed when I hear other people talk
about their problems. I think some people don't

mind it and they even encourage it because they consider themselves to be good at giving advice and helping their friends. When people tell me their problems I often shut down because I feel like I am always held together barely by anything and one more thing could take me down. I think that is shitty.

If you can make it through ten seconds, you can make it through anything. Someone told me that.

You know what this is?

Mama and baby got hit by a car while crossing the road

Sorry,I didn't realize I excluded you

Today 12:01 AM

thats so sad

I know. I cried my eyes out

You know what these are?

Today 12:26 PM

awwww

I love rabbits

same

Welp it looks like putting my everything into one person and praying that true love would solve all my problems didn't work out again

Did you know God makes fields of flowers all the time. Have you ever been in your car at noon in a McDonald's parking lot? everyone eating their food alone in their cars at the same time all next to each other planted in a row?

I fucked God and it made me feel whole.
I have been fucking God for a little bit now. I
think God fucks a lot. God comes to people who
pray, who need to be touched, who he talks to
a lot, who he talks to never. God comes to you
in the form of whatever you need him to be. He
has no genitals. He is also not explicitly a "he"
by any means. I am just writing this from my
point of view. God comes at night when you're
alone in your bed. God comes when you let your
tiny mouth say small words to him, when you're
whispering your hopes and dreams at night
asking for a sign. His big "hands" are so large
that his touch envelops your whole body. When I
was 10, I had a dream I drowned in a pool. I felt
myself unable to reach the surface of the water
and I felt myself die and in the moment after my
death I did not wake up...I floated. I felt what it
was to be aware of death. To be dead and know
it. God makes you float. God makes you feel
what it is to be fucked by God and know it, even
if you're not REALLY being fucked by God.
Nobody enters you. Nobody spreads your legs
apart unless you want. There is no forcing. There
is no aggression, not like the violent myths. God
doesn't fuck like the myths. God fucked me for
the first time when I was 19. I had first started
getting sick and was talking to God everyday.

When you don't feel good, you are so close to God. I was in bed in the fetal position and God wrapped himself around me. I felt him get hard with his crotch pushed against my ass. I felt him hard all over my body though. I felt him hard behind me everywhere. The entire vibrating body God was inhabiting was hot and hard. He held his hardness for a second and then became a rush of hot flowing water. I didn't move, but I felt my insides begin to pulsate and become hot. I felt my head become full of light and felt myself getting ready to cum. I felt my head ascend. I felt my thoughts become flashes of bright lights and I saw his face. I felt my insides clench and I came. My entire body convulsed and tightened and then relaxed. I felt like I had been heated up. As I felt my mind and body return back to Earth, God gave me a kiss on the forehead and told me he'd call me sometime. Oh God, please keep calling.

When asked to be nice, I evoke the spirit of you because you're one of the first people to really show me what it means to be a good person... when I want to feel unashamed I think of you...I think of what you would do, moving unapologet- ically through space and I think about what made me love you to begin with. I can't even believe there was ever a point in which I didn't know we were supposed to be together. Or I wasn't sure. I know it doesn't matter because we are here now where we are supposed to be, but it's funny because now I would never waste another moment that didn't deserve to be wasted

God: You are human. You are part animal and part god.

me: Wow amazing! Imagine all the things that can be accomplished w/ the strength of an animal but the mind of a god.

God: Actually you will be an animal in the way that you will shit and sleep and cry and fuck and be afraid but you will not be strong. You will have back problems. You will feel shame.

me: Ok well at least we get to be part god!

God: You will have no powers. You will only be a god in the sense that you will carry the heavy weight of the questioning of purpose and think a lot about morals and the big picture, but you will have no control.

me: I don't understand how you can let bad things happen to me and my friends? How are you just supposed to expect an addict to not be addicted to the thing that makes them feel good when being sober makes them have to acknowledge the reality they are trying to hide from by getting high...whatever reality they face that they cannot look into so much so that they must get high?

God: I don't expect anything. I have not had a part in humans in a long time. It is not my job to take care of humans. I feel like you're asking me what my plan is, but my plans are very clear in many places. They are clear in places you don't look even though all the signs point to them. The hand of God has made bugs that look like sticks and candy grow from trees and you don't see that that is all it is about. God made this planet and God made the chemical compounds that make up all human life. But God let it all unfold after that. God does not have the power to make consciousness. Consciousness came from years of trial and error, time after time, many new beginnings and although God electrocuted the first primordial soup God did not give the fish legs. Everything that happened after that just simply played by the rules of this newly created universe. I know about as much as you. But I can see from very far away and I can see everyone at once so I get pretty good at knowing everything that goes on and I monitor and intervene sometimes when it just feels right. I can't really explain that part. I have to live my own life too. I make mistakes too. The real lesson is that life is what it is. And I'm sorry for the bad things that happen. This all started very much

as a simple experiment. Some people call it the
greatest experiment that ever existed. I can't
tell you anymore though.

Lauren Cook is a transsexual naturalist and the author of *Sex Goblin* (Nightboat Books, 2024). He is from Upstate New York.

NIGHTBOAT BOOKS

Nightboat Books, a nonprofit organization, seeks to develop audiences for writers whose work resists convention and transcends boundaries. We publish books rich with poignancy, intelligence, and risk. Please visit nightboat.org to learn about our titles and how you can support our future publications.

The following individuals have supported the publication of this book. We thank them for their generosity and commitment to the mission of Nightboat Books:

Kazim Ali
Anonymous (8)
Mary Armantrout
Jean C. Ballantyne
Thomas Ballantyne
Bill Bruns
John Cappetta
V. Shannon Clyne
Ulla Dydo Charitable Fund
Photios Giovanis
Amanda Greenberger
Vandana Khanna
Isaac Klausner
Shari Leinwand
Anne Marie Macari
Elizabeth Madans
Martha Melvoin
Caren Motika
Elizabeth Motika
The Leslie Scalapino - O Books Fund
Robin Shanus
Thomas Shardlow
Rebecca Shea
Ira Silverberg
Benjamin Taylor
David Wall
Jerrie Whitfield & Richard Motika
Arden Wohl
Issam Zineh

This book is made possible, in part, by grants from the New York City Department of Cultural Affairs in partnership with the City Council and the New York State Council on the Arts Literature Program.

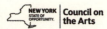